HORRiD HENRY'S
Author Visit

HORRID HENRY'S
Author Visit

Francesca Simon
Illustrated by Tony Ross

Orion
Children's Books

Horrid Henry's Author Visit originally appeared in
Horrid Henry and the Abominable Snowman first published in
Great Britain in 2007 by Orion Children's Books
This edition first published in Great Britain in 2012
by Orion Children's Books
a division of the Orion Publishing Group Ltd
Orion House
5 Upper Saint Martin's Lane
London WC2H 9EA
An Hachette UK Company

1 3 5 7 9 10 8 6 4 2

Text © Francesca Simon 2007, 2012
Illustrations © Tony Ross 2012

ISBN 978 1 4440 0114 3
Printed in China.

www.orionbooks.co.uk
www.horridhenry.co.uk

*For Nigel Bennett
and Eleanor Steyn*

Look out for . . .

There are many more **Horrid Henry** books
available. For a complete list visit
www.horridhenry.co.uk

or

www.orionbooks.co.uk

Contents

Chapter 1

Horrid Henry woke up.

He felt strange.

He felt . . . happy.

He felt . . . excited.

But why?

Was it the weekend?

M	T	W	T	F	S	S
	1	2	3	4	5	6
7	8	9	10	11	12	13
14	15	16	17	18	19	20
21	22	23	24	25	26	27
28	29	30	31			

No.

Was it a day off school?

No.

Had Miss Battle-Axe been kidnapped by aliens and transported to another galaxy to slave in the salt mines?

No (unfortunately).

So why was he feeling so excited
on a school day?

And then Horrid Henry
remembered.

Oh wow!! It was Book Week at Henry's school, and his favourite author in the whole world, TJ Fizz, the writer of the stupendous *Ghost Quest* and *Mad Machines* and *Skeleton Skunks* was coming to talk to his class.

Henry had read every single one
of TJ's brilliant books, even after
lights out.

Rude Ralph thought they were almost as good as Mutant Max comics. Horrid Henry thought they were even better.

Chapter 2

Perfect Peter bounced into Henry's
room.

'Isn't it exciting, Henry?' said Peter. 'Our class is going to meet a real live author! Milksop Miles is coming today. He's the man who wrote *The Happy Nappy*. Do you think he'd sign my copy?'

Horrid Henry snorted.

The Happy Nappy!

Only the dumbest book ever.
All those giant nappies with names
like Rappy Nappy and Zappy Nappy
and Tappy Nappy dancing and
prancing about. And then the truly
horrible Gappy Nappy, who was
always wailing, 'I'm leaking!'

Horrid Henry shuddered.
He was amazed that Milksop Miles
dared to show his face after writing
such a boring book.

'Only a wormy toad like you could like such a stupid story,' said Henry.

'It's not stupid,' said Peter.

'Is too.'

'Is not. And he's bringing his guitar. Miss Lovely said so.'

'Big deal,' said Horrid Henry.
'*We've* got TJ Fizz.'

Perfect Peter shuddered.
'Her books are too scary,' said Peter.

'That's 'cause you're a baby.'

'Mum!' shrieked Peter.

'Henry called me a baby.'

'Telltale,' hissed Henry.

'Don't be horrid, Henry,'
shouted Mum.

Chapter 3

Horrid Henry sat in class with a huge carrier bag filled with all his TJ Fizz books.

Everyone in the class had drawn book covers for *Ghost Quest* and *Ghouls' Jewels*, and written their own *Skeleton Skunk* story.

Henry's of course was the best:

He would give it to TJ Fizz if
she paid him a million pounds.

Ten minutes to go.

How could he live until it was time
for her to arrive?

Miss Battle-Axe cleared her throat.
'Class, we have a very important
guest coming. I know you're all
very excited, but I will not tolerate
anything but perfect behaviour today.
Anyone who misbehaves will be
sent out. Is that clear?'
She glared at Henry.

Henry scowled back.
Of course he would be perfect.
TJ Fizz was coming!

'Has everyone thought of a good question to ask her? I'll write the best ones on the board,' continued Miss Battle-Axe.

'How much money do you make?' shouted Rude Ralph.

'How many TVs do you have?'
shouted Horrid Henry.

'Do you like fudge?'
shouted Greedy Graham.

'I said *good* questions,' snapped
Miss Battle-Axe. 'Bert, what's your
question for TJ Fizz?'

'I dunno,' said Beefy Bert.

Rumble.

Rumble.

Rumble.

Ooops. Henry's tummy was telling
him it was snacktime.

It must be all the excitement.
It was strictly forbidden
to eat in class, but Henry was
a master sneaker.

He certainly wouldn't want his
tummy to gurgle while
TJ Fizz was talking.

Chapter 4

Miss Battle-Axe was writing down
Clever Clare's eight questions
on the board.

Slowly, carefully, silently,
Horrid Henry opened his lunchbox
under the table.

Slowly, carefully, silently, he eased
open the bag of crisps.

Horrid Henry looked to the left.
Rude Ralph was waving his hand
in the air.

Horrid Henry looked to the right.
Greedy Graham was drooling and
opening a bag of sweets.

The coast was clear. Henry popped some Super Spicy Hedgehog crisps into his mouth.

MUNCH!

CRUNCH!

'C'mon, Henry, give me some
crisps,' whispered Rude Ralph.

'No,' hissed Horrid Henry.
'Eat your own.'

'I'm starving,' moaned Greedy Graham. 'Gimme a crisp.'

'No!' hissed Horrid Henry.

MUNCH CRUNCH YANK

Huh?

Miss Battle-Axe towered over him holding aloft his bag of crisps. Her red eyes were like two icy daggers.

'What did I tell you, Henry?'
said Miss Battle-Axe.
'No bad behaviour would be
tolerated. Go to Miss Lovely's class.'

'But … but … TJ Fizz is coming,'
spluttered Henry.
'I was just . . .'

Miss Battle-Axe pointed to the door.
'Out!'

'NOOOOOOOOOO!'

howled Henry.

Chapter 5

Horrid Henry sat in a tiny chair at
the back of Miss Lovely's room.
Never had he suffered such torment.
He tried to block his ears as Milksop
Miles read his horrible book to
Peter's class.

'Hello, Happy, Clappy and Yappy!
Can *you* find the leak?'

'No,' said Happy.

'No,' said Clappy.

'No,' said Yappy.

'I can,' said Gappy Nappy.

AAAARRRRGGGGGHHH!

Horrid Henry gritted his teeth.

He would go mad having to listen
to this a moment longer.
He had to get out of here.

'All together now, let's sing the Happy Nappy song,' trilled Milksop Miles, whipping out his guitar.

'Yay!' cheered the infants.

No, groaned Henry.

Oh I'm a happy nappy,

 a happy zappy nappy

I wrap up your bottom,
snug and tight,

And keep you dry all through
the night

Oh –

53

This was torture.

No, this was
worse than torture.

How could he sit here listening to
the horrible Happy Nappy song
knowing that just above him
TJ Fizz was reading from one of her
incredible books, passing round the
famous skunk skeleton, and showing
off her *Ghost Quest* drawings.

He had to get back to his own class.
He had to. But how?

What if he joined in the singing?
He could bellow:

Oh I'm a soggy nappy
A smelly, stinky nappy –

Yes! That would certainly get him
sent out the door straight to —
the head.

Not back to his class and TJ Fizz.
Horrid Henry closed his mouth.

Rats.

Maybe there'd be an earthquake?
A power failure? Where was a
fire-drill when you needed one?

He could always pretend he needed
the toilet. But then when he didn't
come back they'd come looking
for him.

Or maybe he could just sneak away?
Why not? Henry got to his feet and
began to slide towards the door,
trying to be invisible.

Sneak, Sneak, Sn . . .

'Whooa, come back here, little boy,'
shouted Milksop Miles, twanging
his guitar. Henry froze.
'Our party is just starting. Now who
knows the Happy Nappy dance?'

'I do,' said
Perfect Peter.

'I do,' said
Goody–Goody
Gordon.

'We all do,'
said Tidy Ted.

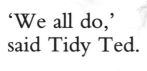

'Everyone on their feet,'
said Milksop Miles. 'Ah-one, ah-two,
let's all do the Nappy Dance!'

'Nap nap nap nap nap nap nappy,'
warbled Miles.

'Nap nap nap nap nap nap nappy,'
warbled Peter's class, dancing away.

Desperate times call for
desperate measures.

Horrid Henry started dancing.

Slowly, he tapped his way closer and closer and closer to the door and – freedom!

Chapter 6

Horrid Henry reached for the door knob. Miss Lovely was busy dancing in the corner.

Just a few more steps...

'Who's going to be my little helper
while we act out the story?'
beamed Miles. 'Who would like
to play the Happy Nappy?'

'Me! Me!'
squealed Miss Lovely's class.

Horrid Henry sank against the wall.

'Come on, don't be shy,' said Miles,
pointing straight at Henry.
'Come on up and put on the magic
happy nappy!'

And he marched over and dangled
an enormous blue nappy in front
of Henry. It was over one metre
wide and one metre high, with
a hideous smiling face and
big goggly eyes.

Horrid Henry took a step back.
He felt faint.

The giant nappy was looming above
him. In a moment it would be over
his head and he'd be trapped inside.
His name would be mud – forever.

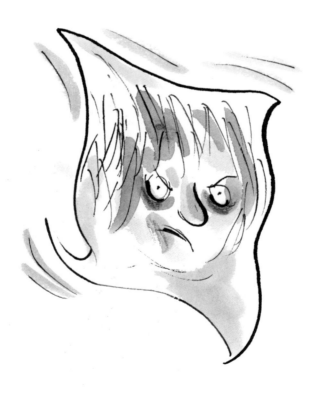

Henry the nappy.
Henry the giant nappy.
Henry the giant happy nappy . . .

'AAAARRRRGGGGGHHH!'

screamed Horrid Henry.
'Get away from me!'

Milksop Miles stopped waving
the gigantic nappy. 'Oh dear,' he said.

'Oh dear,' said Miss Lovely.

'Don't be scared,' said Miles.

Scared? Horrid Henry … scared?
Of a giant nappy? Henry opened
his mouth to scream. And then
he stopped. What if…?

'Help! Help! I'm being attacked
by a nappy!' screeched Henry.

'HELLLLLLLLP!'

Milksop Miles looked at Miss Lovely.
Miss Lovely looked at Milksop Miles.

'HELLLLLLLP!
HELLLLLLLP!'

'Henry? Are you OK?'
piped Perfect Peter.

'NOOOOOOOO!'
wailed Horrid Henry, cowering.
'I'm … I'm … nappy-phobic.'

'Never mind,' said Milksop Miles. 'You're not the first boy who's been scared of a giant nappy.'

'I'm sure I'll be fine if I go back to my own class,' gasped Horrid Henry.

Miss Lovely hesitated. Horrid Henry opened his mouth to howl.

'Run along then,' said Miss Lovely quickly.

Horrid Henry did not wait to be
asked twice. He raced out of Miss
Lovely's class, then dashed upstairs
to his own. *Skeleton Skunk* here
I come, thought Henry,
bursting through the door.

There was the great and glorious
TJ Fizz, just about to start reading
a brand new chapter from her
latest book, *Skeleton Stinkbomb*.
Hallelujah, he was on time.

'Henry, what are you doing here?'
hissed Miss Battle-Axe.

'Miss Lovely sent me back,' beamed Horrid Henry. 'And you did say we should be on our best behaviour today, so I did what I was told.'

Henry sat down as TJ began to read. The story was amazing. Ahhh, sighed Horrid Henry happily, wasn't life grand?